The Taming of the Shrew

William Shakespeare

SADDLEBACK
EDUCATIONAL PUBLISHING

Saddleback's *Illustrated Classics*™

SADDLEBACK
EDUCATIONAL PUBLISHING
www.sdlback.com

ISBN-13: 978-1-59905-155-0
ISBN-10: 1-59905-155-9
eBook: 978-1-60291-182-6

Printed in Guangzhou, China
NOR/0313/CA21300401

17 16 15 14 13   5 6 7 8 9 10

Welcome to
Saddleback's *Illustrated Classics*™

We are proud to welcome you to Saddleback's *Illustrated Classics*™. Saddleback's *Illustrated Classics*™ was designed specifically for the classroom to introduce readers to many of the great classics in literature. Each text, written and adapted by teachers and researchers, has been edited using the Dale-Chall vocabulary system. In addition, much time and effort has been spent to ensure that these high-interest stories retain all of the excitement, intrigue, and adventure of the original books.

With these graphically *Illustrated Classics*™, you learn what happens in the story in a number of different ways. One way is by reading the words a character says. Another way is by looking at the drawings of the character. The artist can tell you what kind of person a character is and what he or she is thinking or feeling.

This series will help you to develop confidence and a sense of accomplishment as you finish each novel. The stories in Saddleback's *Illustrated Classics*™ are fun to read. And remember, fun motivates!

Overview

Everyone deserves to read the best literature our language has to offer. Saddleback's *Illustrated Classics*™ was designed to acquaint readers with the most famous stories from the world's greatest authors, while teaching essential skills. You will learn how to:

- Establish a purpose for reading
- Activate prior knowledge
- Evaluate your reading
- Listen to the language as it is written
- Extend literary and language appreciation through discussion and writing activities.

Reading is one of the most important skills you will ever learn. It provides the key to all kinds of information. By reading the *Illustrated Classics*™, you will develop confidence and the self-satisfaction that comes from accomplishment—a solid foundation for any reader.

Remember,

"Today's readers are tomorrow's leaders."

William Shakespeare

William Shakespeare was baptized on April 26, 1564, in Stratford-on-Avon, England, the third child of John Shakespeare, a well-to-do merchant, and Mary Arden, his wife. Young William probably attended the Stratford grammar school, where he learned English, Greek, and a great deal of Latin. Historians aren't sure of the exact date of Shakespeare's birth.

In 1582, Shakespeare married Anne Hathaway. By 1583 the couple had a daughter, Susanna, and two years later the twins, Hamnet and Judith. Somewhere between 1585 and 1592 Shakespeare went to London, where he became first an actor and then a playwright. His acting company, *The King's Men*, appeared most often in the *Globe* theater, a part of which Shakespeare himself owned.

In all, Shakespeare is believed to have written thirty-seven plays, several nondramatic poems, and a number of sonnets. In 1611 when he left the active life of the theater, he returned to Stratford and became a country gentleman, living in the second-largest house in town. For five years he lived a quiet life. Then, on April 23, 1616, William Shakespeare died and was buried in Trinity Church in Stratford. From his own time to the present, Shakespeare is considered one of the greatest writers of the English-speaking world.

William Shakespeare

The Taming of the Shrew

BIANCA

LUCENTO

KATHERINA

BAPTISTA

VINCENTIO

PETRUCHIO

THIS IS A STORY OF TWO YOUNG WOMEN, ONE SWEET AND GENTLE, THE OTHER A SHREW.* ONE MARRIES FOR LOVE, THE OTHER FOR MONEY. WHO IS HAPPIER? THE ANSWER MAY SURPRISE YOU!

* an arguing, scolding woman with a fiery temper

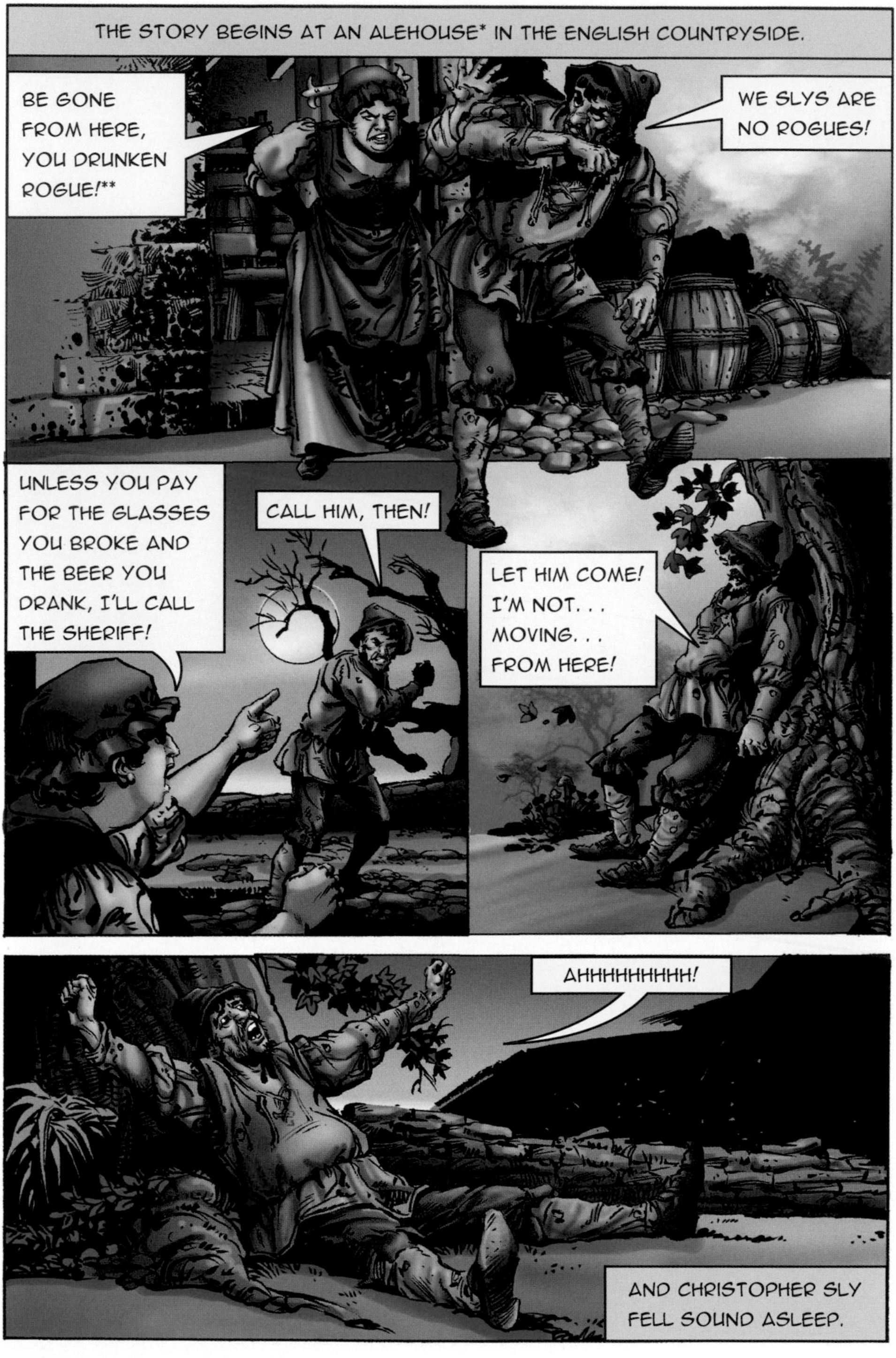
THE STORY BEGINS AT AN ALEHOUSE* IN THE ENGLISH COUNTRYSIDE.
BE GONE FROM HERE, YOU DRUNKEN ROGUE!**
WE SLYS ARE NO ROGUES!
UNLESS YOU PAY FOR THE GLASSES YOU BROKE AND THE BEER YOU DRANK, I'LL CALL THE SHERIFF!
CALL HIM, THEN!
LET HIM COME! I'M NOT. . . MOVING. . . FROM HERE!
AHHHHHHHHH!
AND CHRISTOPHER SLY FELL SOUND ASLEEP.

* tavern

** tramp

AS CHRISTOPHER SLY SLEPT, A NOBLEMAN* AND HIS SERVANTS WERE RETURNING FROM A HUNT.

WHAT'S THIS? IS HE DEAD OR DRUNK?

ASLEEP, SIR. HE'D BE VERY COLD IF HE WERE NOT WARMED WITH BEER!

I HAVE IN MIND A JOKE TO PLAY ON THIS BEGGAR!

TAKE HIM TO MY HOME.

* a wealthy man of high rank

WASH HIM AND DRESS HIM AND PUT HIM TO BED IN MY BEST BEDROOM.

HAVE SOFT MUSIC PLAYED, AND INCENSE* BURNED ON THE FIRE TO MAKE THE AIR SWEET!

IT WILL SEEM STRANGE TO HIM WHEN HE WAKES UP!

WHEN HE *DOES* WAKE UP, YOU MUST BOW LOW TO HIM AND SAY, "WHAT CAN I DO FOR YOU, SIR?"

SAY THAT HE ONLY DREAMS HE IS CHRISTOPHER SLY. . . THAT HE IS REALLY A NOBLEMAN!

WE WILL PLAY OUR PART.

* a sweet-smelling powder

AS THE SERVANTS TOOK SLY AWAY, A GROUP OF ACTORS ARRIVED.

WE ARE ACTORS WHO WANT TO PERFORM FOR YOU!

AND WHO ARE YOU?

TAKE THEM TO MY HOUSE. MAKE THEM WELCOME.

YOU COME AT A GOOD TIME. YOU CAN HELP WITH A JOKE I HAVE UNDER WAY!

WE THANK YOU!

YES, SIR.

THE ORDERS WERE CARRIED OUT. LATER, SLY AWOKE IN A FINE BEDROOM.

WHERE AM I?

A GLASS OF WINE FOR YOU, SIR?

MAY I SHAVE YOU, SIR?

WHICH CLOTHES WILL YOU WEAR TODAY?

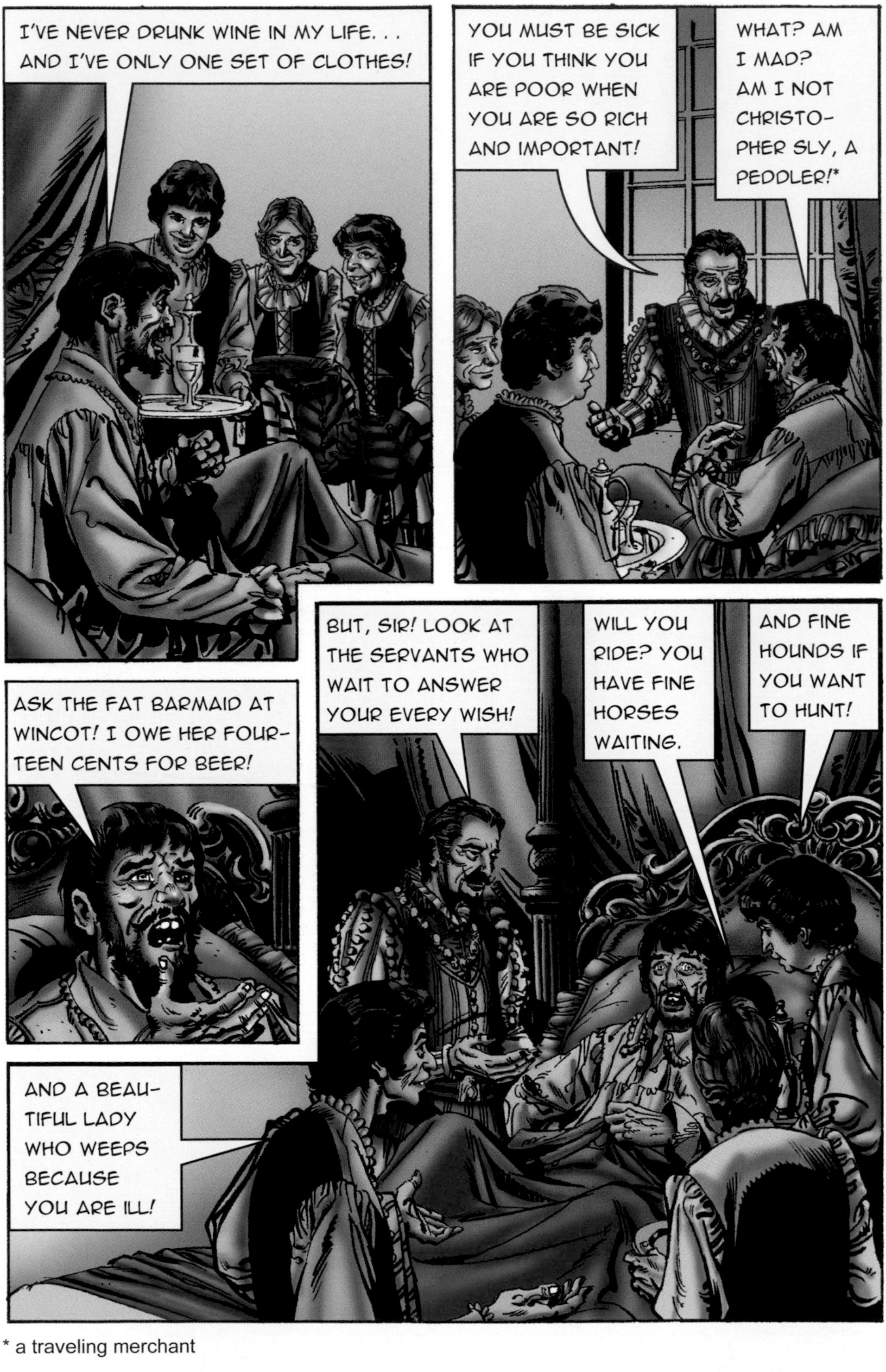
I'VE NEVER DRUNK WINE IN MY LIFE. . . AND I'VE ONLY ONE SET OF CLOTHES!
YOU MUST BE SICK IF YOU THINK YOU ARE POOR WHEN YOU ARE SO RICH AND IMPORTANT!
WHAT? AM I MAD? AM I NOT CHRISTO-PHER SLY, A PEDDLER!*
ASK THE FAT BARMAID AT WINCOT! I OWE HER FOUR-TEEN CENTS FOR BEER!
BUT, SIR! LOOK AT THE SERVANTS WHO WAIT TO ANSWER YOUR EVERY WISH!
WILL YOU RIDE? YOU HAVE FINE HORSES WAITING.
AND FINE HOUNDS IF YOU WANT TO HUNT!
AND A BEAU-TIFUL LADY WHO WEEPS BECAUSE YOU ARE ILL!

* a traveling merchant

IS IT TRUE? I'M NOT DREAMING? I FEEL THIS HOT WATER!

WHY... I *AM* A RICH MAN! BRING MY LADY HERE! AND A MUG OF BEER!

YOUR MIND IS WELL AGAIN! FOR SO MANY YEARS YOU'VE DREAMED YOU WERE A POOR MAN!

HOW *ARE* YOU, MY NOBLE HUSBAND?

I AM WELL, NOW THAT YOU ARE HERE!

SLY WAS DRESSED AS A NOBLEMAN. THEN A PAGE* ENTERED, DRESSED AS HIS LADY.

NOBLE SIR, YOUR DOCTORS THINK THAT YOU SHOULD SEE A PLAY. FUN AND LAUGHTER WILL HELP TO CURE YOU.

WE WILL SEE IT.

* young male servant

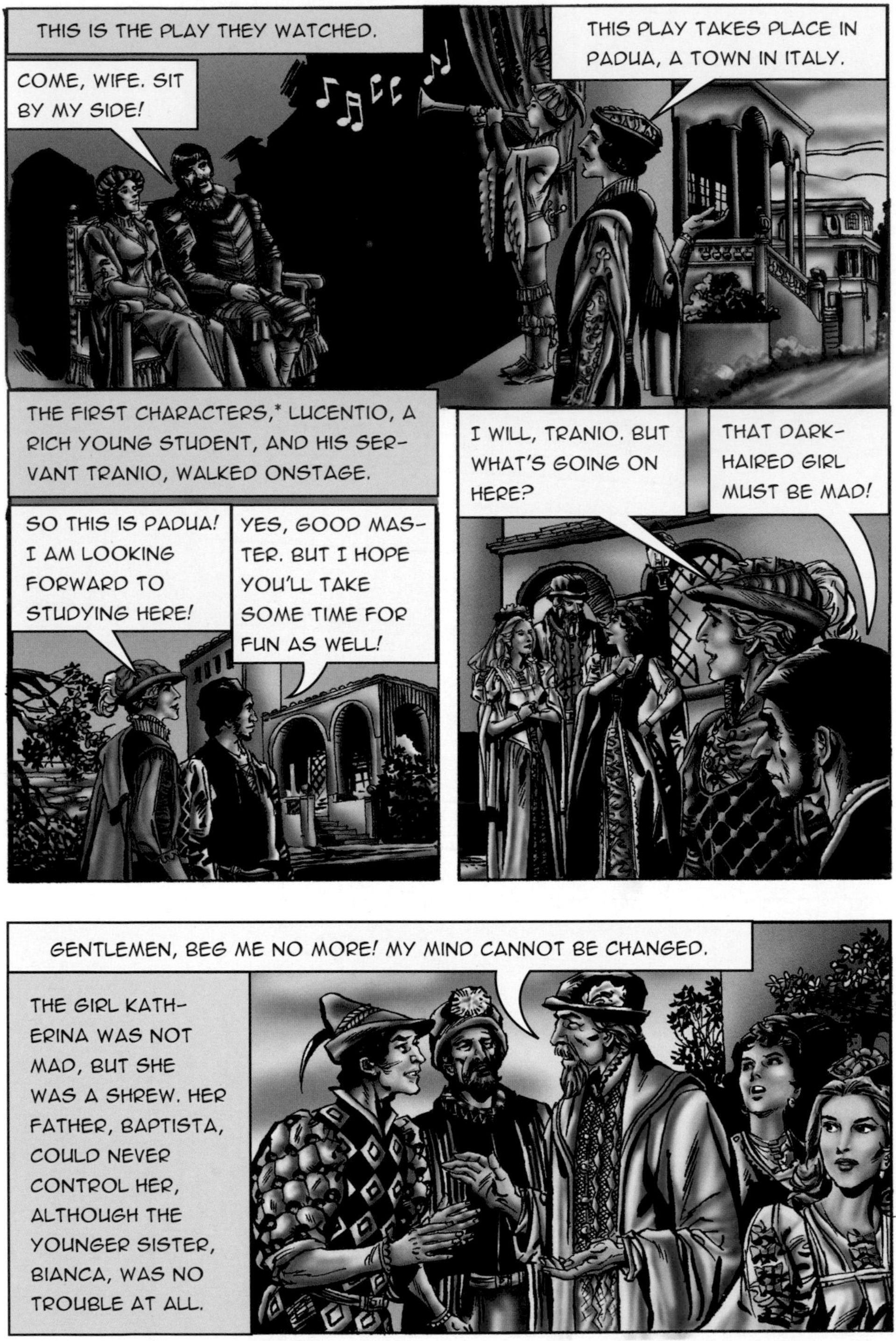
THIS IS THE PLAY THEY WATCHED.
COME, WIFE. SIT BY MY SIDE!
THIS PLAY TAKES PLACE IN PADUA, A TOWN IN ITALY.
THE FIRST CHARACTERS,* LUCENTIO, A RICH YOUNG STUDENT, AND HIS SERVANT TRANIO, WALKED ONSTAGE.
SO THIS IS PADUA! I AM LOOKING FORWARD TO STUDYING HERE!
YES, GOOD MASTER. BUT I HOPE YOU'LL TAKE SOME TIME FOR FUN AS WELL!
I WILL, TRANIO. BUT WHAT'S GOING ON HERE?
THAT DARK-HAIRED GIRL MUST BE MAD!
GENTLEMEN, BEG ME NO MORE! MY MIND CANNOT BE CHANGED.
THE GIRL KATHERINA WAS NOT MAD, BUT SHE WAS A SHREW. HER FATHER, BAPTISTA, COULD NEVER CONTROL HER, ALTHOUGH THE YOUNGER SISTER, BIANCA, WAS NO TROUBLE AT ALL.

* actors in a play

SIGNIOR* GREMIO AND SIGNIOR HORTENSIO, I AM SORRY. BUT I WILL NOT ALLOW MY YOUNGEST DAUGHTER TO MARRY UNTIL MY OLDEST, KATHERINA, IS WED!

BUT, SIR!

WE'LL GO HOME, NOW, BIANCA. THINGS WILL WORK OUT.

YES, FATHER. BOOKS AND MUSIC SHALL KEEP ME COMPANY.

IT'S NOT FAIR TO LOCK HER UP LIKE THAT!

DON'T WORRY. I WILL TAKE CARE OF HER!

I WILL PAY HIGH SALARIES** FOR THE BEST TEACHERS FOR HER! IF YOU KNOW ANY SEND THEM TO ME.

* sir, Mr.

** wages, money earned for work

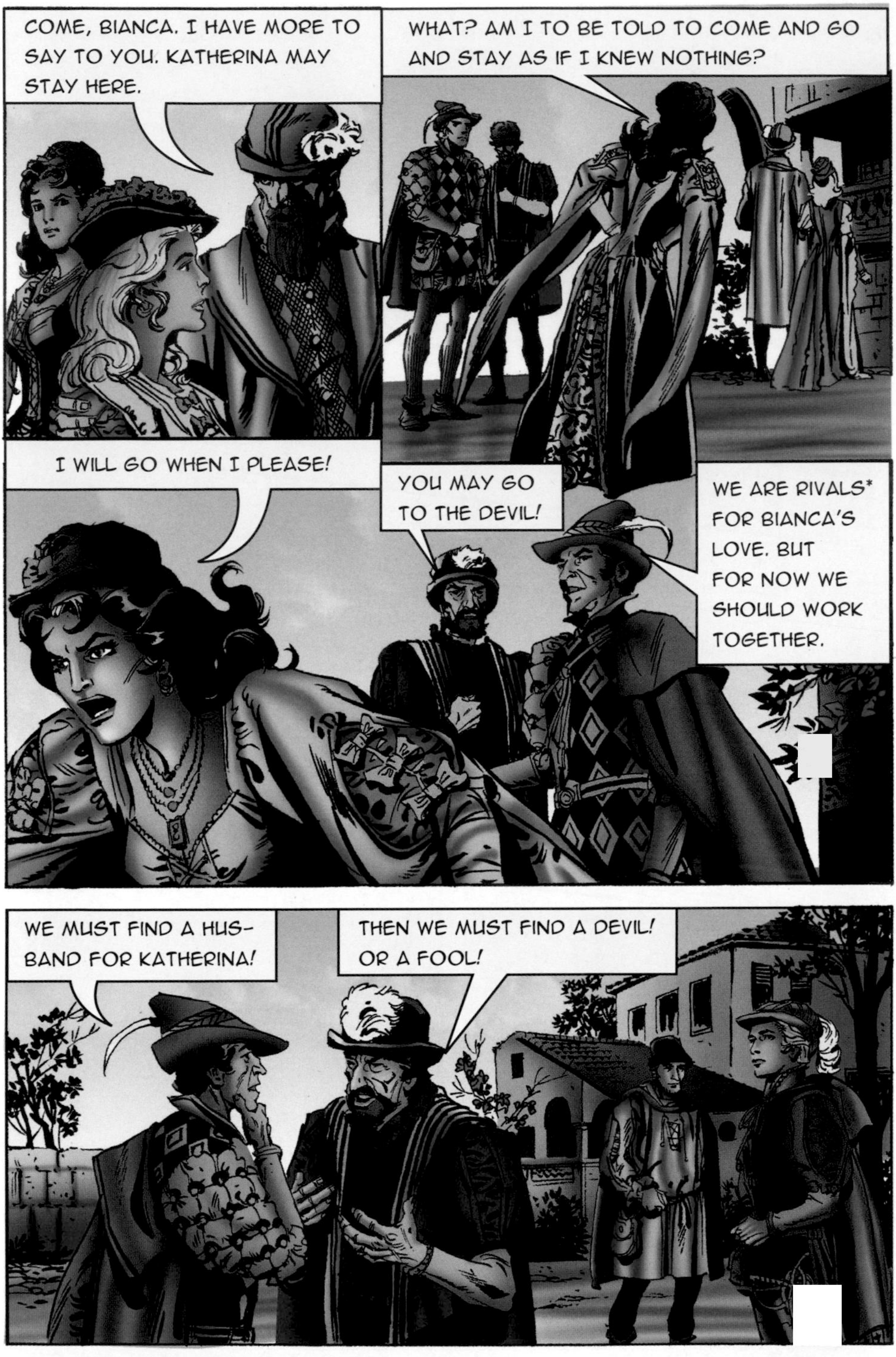
COME, BIANCA. I HAVE MORE TO SAY TO YOU. KATHERINA MAY STAY HERE.
WHAT? AM I TO BE TOLD TO COME AND GO AND STAY AS IF I KNEW NOTHING?
I WILL GO WHEN I PLEASE!
YOU MAY GO TO THE DEVIL!
WE ARE RIVALS* FOR BIANCA'S LOVE. BUT FOR NOW WE SHOULD WORK TOGETHER.
WE MUST FIND A HUS- BAND FOR KATHERINA!
THEN WE MUST FIND A DEVIL! OR A FOOL!

* two people who fight each other to obtain something

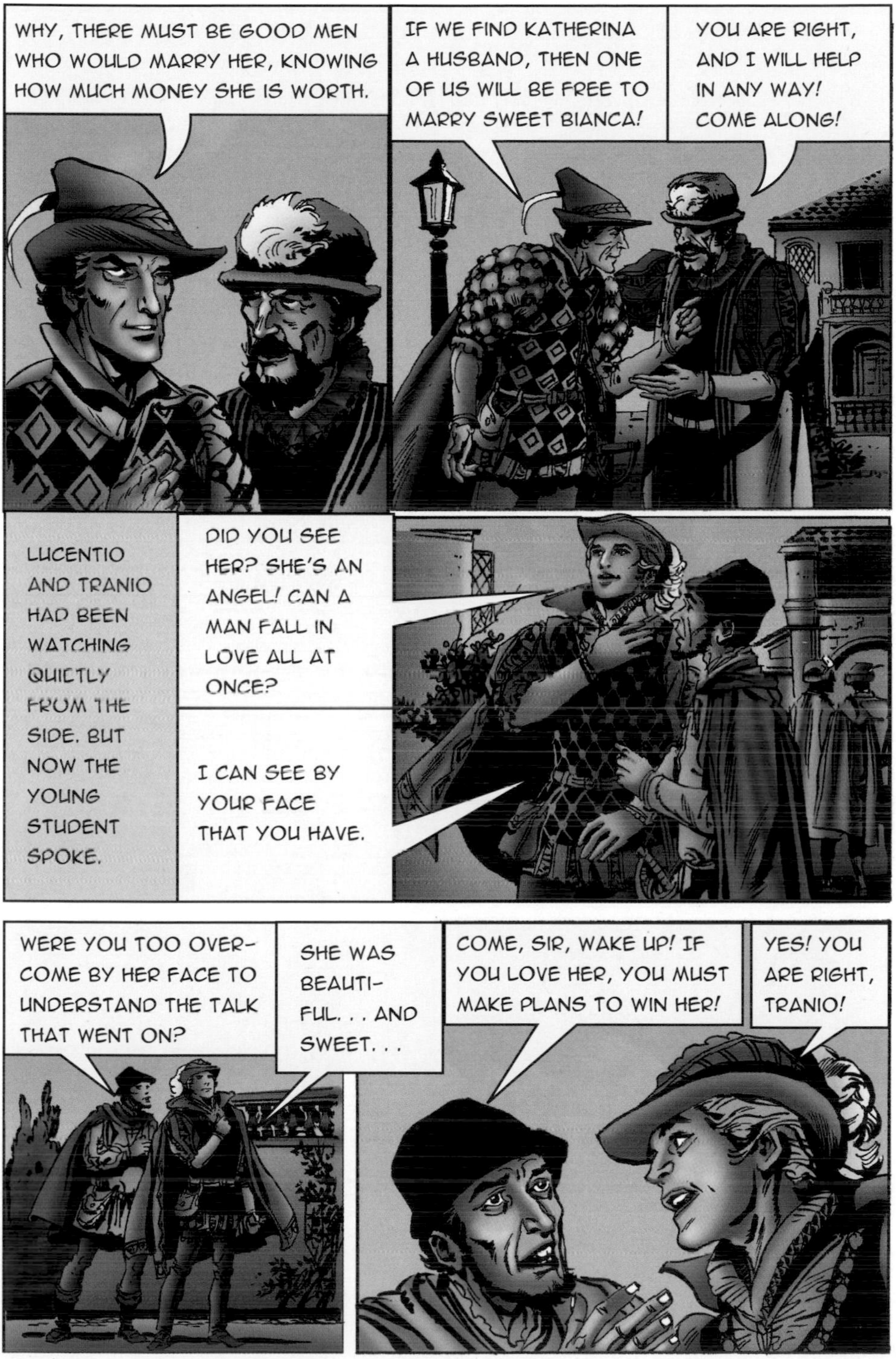
WHY, THERE MUST BE GOOD MEN WHO WOULD MARRY HER, KNOWING HOW MUCH MONEY SHE IS WORTH.
IF WE FIND KATHERINA A HUSBAND, THEN ONE OF US WILL BE FREE TO MARRY SWEET BIANCA!
YOU ARE RIGHT, AND I WILL HELP IN ANY WAY! COME ALONG!
LUCENTIO AND TRANIO HAD BEEN WATCHING QUIETLY FROM THE SIDE. BUT NOW THE YOUNG STUDENT SPOKE.
DID YOU SEE HER? SHE'S AN ANGEL! CAN A MAN FALL IN LOVE ALL AT ONCE?
I CAN SEE BY YOUR FACE THAT YOU HAVE.
WERE YOU TOO OVER-COME BY HER FACE TO UNDERSTAND THE TALK THAT WENT ON?
SHE WAS BEAUTI-FUL. . . AND SWEET. . .
COME, SIR, WAKE UP! IF YOU LOVE HER, YOU MUST MAKE PLANS TO WIN HER!
YES! YOU ARE RIGHT, TRANIO!

THE OLDER SISTER IS SO BAD-TEMPERED THAT UNTIL SHE IS OFF HIS HANDS, THE FATHER WILL KEEP YOUR LOVED ONE SHUT UP AT HOME!

CRUEL! BUT DID HE NOT SAY HE WOULD GET SCHOOLMASTERS TO TEACH HER?

THAT'S RIGHT! AND NOW WE HAVE OUR PLAN.

YES, I SEE! I WILL BE THE SCHOOL MASTER AND TEACH SWEET BIANCA!

BUT CAN IT BE DONE? YOU MUST MEET YOUR FATHER'S FRIENDS HERE, ENTERTAIN THEM, DO BUSINESS FOR HIM.

NO ONE HERE KNOWS US. YOU WILL TAKE MY PLACE! YOU WILL BE THE MASTER!

QUICK! CHANGE HATS AND CLOAKS WITH ME!

WELL. . . YOUR FATHER TOLD ME TO SERVE AND OBEY YOU.

BIONDELLO, ANOTHER SERVANT OF LUCENTIO'S RUSHED UP TO THEM.

HAS TRANIO STOLEN MY MASTER'S CLOTHES?

TRANIO HAS CHANGED CLOTHES WITH ME TO SAVE MY LIFE!

BY ACCIDENT I KILLED A MAN IN A QUARREL! TRANIO WILL ACT LIKE ME WHILE I ESCAPE. YOU UNDERSTAND?

N-NO, SIR!

YOU WILL WAIT ON TRANIO AS IF HE WERE I . . . AND NOT A WORD OF THIS TO ANYONE!

Y-YES, SIR.

AS LUCENTIO LEFT, PETRUCHIO, ALSO NEW IN PADUA, ARRIVED WITH HIS SERVANT GRUMIO.

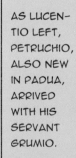

THIS SHOULD BE MY GOOD FRIEND HORTENSIO'S HOUSE. KNOCK, GRUMIO!

KNOCK, SIR? KNOCK WHO? YOU OR AN ENEMY!

KNOCK AT THE GATE, STUPID, OR I WILL KNOCK YOUR HEAD.

ALL RIGHT, MASTER, BUT WHY NOT SAY WHAT YOU MEAN?

JUST THEN, HORTENSIO APPEARED.

MY DEAR FRIEND PETRUCHIO—AND GRUMIO! WHAT HAPPY WIND BLOWS YOU TO PADUA?

SUCH WIND AS SENDS YOUNG MEN OUT TO SEEK THEIR FORTUNES!

MY FATHER HAS DIED. I HAVE MONEY IN MY PURSE, PROPERTY AT HOME, AND I COME TO SEEK A WIFE!

I COULD FIND YOU ONE WHO WILL BE RICH, VERY RICH! BUT YOU ARE TOO GOOD A FRIEND. I CAN'T DO THAT TO YOU.

THIS WOMAN IS A SHREW. YOU WOULD NOT THANK ME FOR HER.

IF SHE IS RICH ENOUGH, I WOULD THANK YOU, NO MATTER WHAT ELSE SHE IS!

GIVE HIM GOLD ENOUGH, AND HE'LL MARRY AN OLD HAG WITHOUT A TOOTH IN HER HEAD!

WELL, SHE *IS* RICH AND YOUNG AND BEAUTIFUL—BUT SO BAD-TEMPERED THAT EVEN *I* WOULD NOT MARRY HER FOR A GOLD MINE!

TELL ME HER FATHER'S NAME.

HE IS BAPTISTA MINOLA, A GENTLEMAN. SHE IS KATHERINA MINOLA, KNOWN FOR HER SCOLDING TONGUE!

I KNOW HER FATHER. . . HE KNEW MY FATHER WELL. I WON'T SLEEP UNTIL I SEE THIS WOMAN!

YOU DON'T KNOW MY MASTER, SIGNIOR HORTENSIO. THIS GIRL DOESN'T STAND A CHANCE! SCOLDING WILL DO HER NO GOOD, FOR HE CAN OUT-SCOLD *ANYONE*.

COME, TAKE ME TO HER!

WAIT, PETRU-CHIO!

BIANCA, KATHERINA'S YOUNGER SISTER, IS THE LOVE OF MY LIFE!

BUT UNTIL KATHERINA IS MARRIED, HER FATHER WON'T ALLOW ANYONE TO COURT HER!

SO, DEAR FRIEND, YOU CAN DO ME A FAVOR!

TAKE ME WITH YOU. INTRODUCE* ME TO BAPTISTA AS A MUSIC TEACHER FOR BIANCA!

SO THAT YOU WILL HAVE A CHANCE TO SEE BIANCA! OF COURSE I WILL!

ON THE WAY TO BAPTISTA'S HOUSE THEY MET GREMIO. THE OLD MAN HAD COME UPON LUCENTIO DISGUISED** AS A SCHOOLMASTER AND WAS BRINGING HIM TO BAPTISTA.

WAIT, PETRUCHIO! HERE IS MY RIVAL FOR BIANCA'S LOVE.

AH, SIGNIOR HORTENSIO!

* to allow two people to meet one another
** made to look like someone else

I HAVE FOUND A TEACHER FOR BIANCA. THIS YOUNG MAN, CAMBIO, CAN INSTRUCT HER IN LITERATURE.

GOOD! AND I HAVE FOUND SOMEONE TO TEACH HER MUSIC.

MORE IMPORTANT, I HAVE FOUND A FRIEND WHO WISHES TO MARRY KATHERINA AND HER DOWRY!*

HAVE YOU TOLD HIM *ALL* HER FAULTS?

I KNOW SHE IS A SHREW. THAT'S NO PROBLEM!

I HAVE HEARD LIONS ROAR, AND THE WILD SEA BEAT AGAINST THE ROCKS!

I'VE HEARD GREAT CANNONS IN THE FIELD OF WAR, AND THUNDER RAGE IN THE SKY!

A WOMAN'S TONGUE CAN'T FRIGHTEN ME!

* the money and property a young woman received from her parents when she married

IT IS LUCKY THIS GENTLEMAN HAS COME HERE, FOR HIS SAKE *AND* OURS!

THEN TRANIO ARRIVED, DRESSED AS LUCENTIO. BIONDELLO FOLLOWED!

GREETINGS, SIRS! PLEASE TELL ME THE WAY TO THE HOUSE OF SIGNIOR BAPTISTA MINOLA.

THE ONE WITH THE TWO BEAUTIFUL DAUGHTERS!

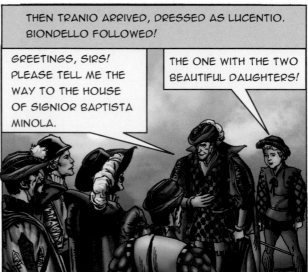

SIR—ARE YOU A SUITOR* OF ONE OF THE DAUGHTERS?

WHAT'S WRONG WITH THAT?

THE YOUNG- EST DAUGHTER, BIANCA, IS LOVED BY MYSELF, SIN- IOR GREMIO!

AND BY MYSELF, SIGNIOR HORTENSIO.

AND THE OLDER DAUGHTER IS FOR ME!

THEN I WILL JOIN THE SUITORS OF BIANCA! LET US EAT AND DRINK TOGETHER AS FRIENDLY RIVALS!

* someone planning to marry

MEANWHILE, IN BAPTISTA'S HOUSE. . .

GOOD SISTER, PLEASE UNTIE MY HANDS! ANYTHING I OWN I WILL GLADLY GIVE YOU!

TELL ME WHICH OF YOUR SUITORS YOU LOVE BEST.

BELIEVE ME, I'VE NOT YET SEEN THAT SPECIAL PERSON.

YOU LIE! IT'S HORTENSIO, ISN'T IT?

NO, NO! IF YOU PREFER HIM, SISTER, YOU SHALL HAVE HIM!

THEN IT'S GREMIO AND HIS RICHES YOU WANT!

JUST THEN BAPTISTA ENTERED THE ROOM.

KATHERINA! WHAT ARE YOU DOING? WHY DO YOU TREAT YOUR SISTER SO BADLY?

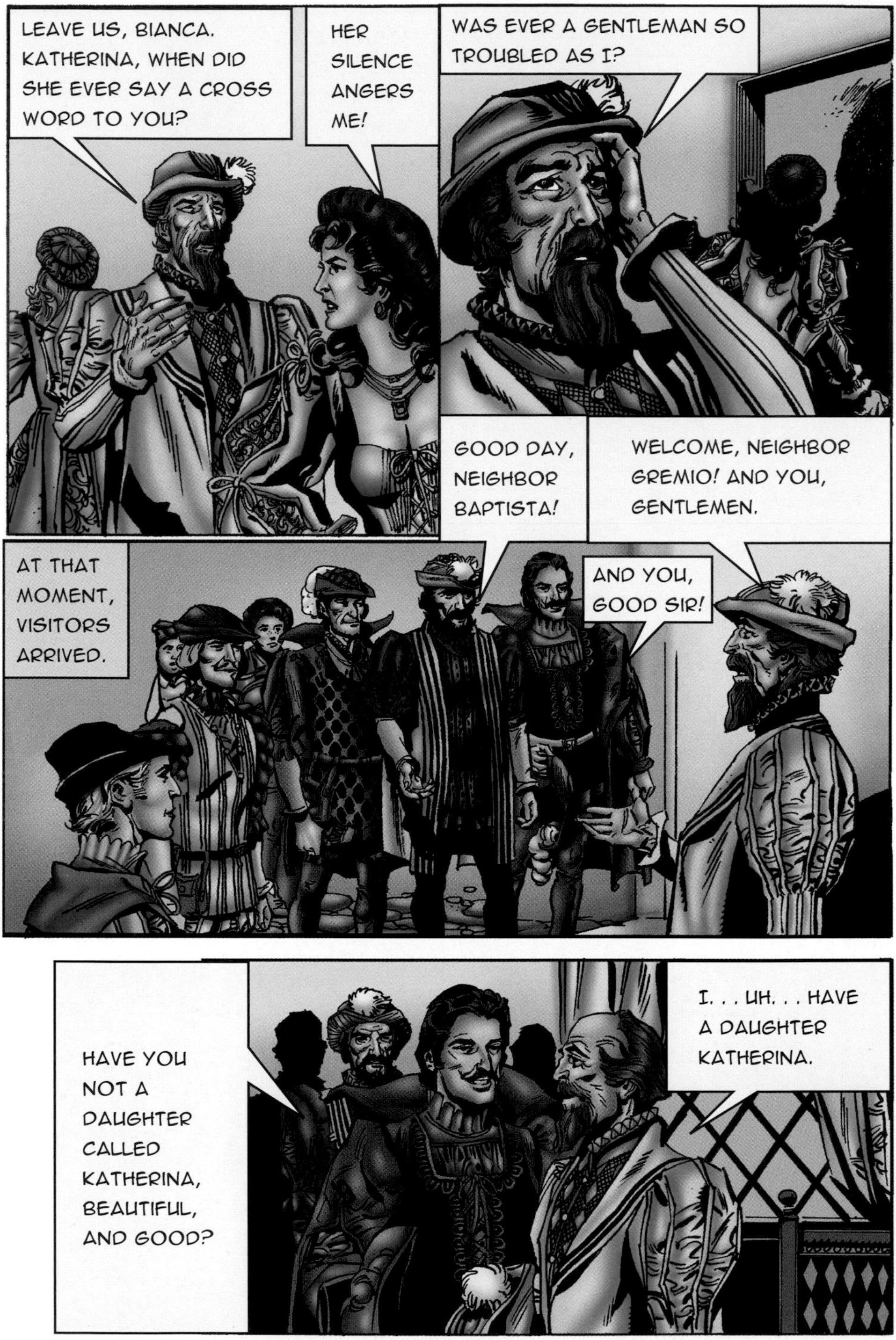
LEAVE US, BIANCA. KATHERINA, WHEN DID SHE EVER SAY A CROSS WORD TO YOU?
HER SILENCE ANGERS ME!
WAS EVER A GENTLEMAN SO TROUBLED AS I?
AT THAT MOMENT, VISITORS ARRIVED.
GOOD DAY, NEIGHBOR BAPTISTA!
WELCOME, NEIGHBOR GREMIO! AND YOU, GENTLEMEN.
AND YOU, GOOD SIR!
HAVE YOU NOT A DAUGHTER CALLED KATHERINA, BEAUTIFUL, AND GOOD?
I. . . UH. . . HAVE A DAUGHTER KATHERINA.

I AM A GENTLE-MAN OF VERONA NAMED PETRUCHIO, ANTONIO'S SON!

I KNEW HIM WELL. YOU ARE WELCOME FOR HIS SAKE!

HAVING HEARD OF YOUR KATHERINA'S GREAT BEAUTY, WIT, AND GOOD NATURE, I HAVE COME TO SEE HER FOR MYSELF.

TO EARN MY WELCOME, I OFFER YOU SOMEONE TO TEACH HER MUSIC AND MATHEMATICS. HIS NAME IS LICIO.

THANK YOU. BUT I FEAR MY KATHERINA WILL NOT SUIT YOU!

THEN PETRUCHIO PRESENTED HORTENSIO DISGUISED AS LICIO, A MUSIC TEACHER.

PLEASE, PETRUCHIO, LET OTHERS SPEAK! I, TOO, HAVE GIFT TO OFFER BAPTISTA.

YOUR PARDON, SIGNIOR GREMIO!

I OFFER YOU THIS YOUNG STUDENT OF GREEK, LATIN, AND OTHER LANGUAGES. PLEASE ACCEPT HIS SERVICES. HIS NAME IS CAMBIO.

A THOUSAND THANKS, GREMIO! WELCOME, GOOD CAMBIO.

AND YOU, GOOD SIR, YOU ARE A STRANGER HERE?

YES. . . I ASK TO BECOME ONE OF THE SUITORS OF YOUR DAUGHTER BIANCA. I AM LUCENTIO, SON OF VINCENTIO OF PISA.

I HAVE HEARD GREAT THINGS OF HIM! YOU ARE VERY WELCOME HERE.

AND FOR YOUR DAUGHTERS' EDUCATION I OFFER THIS MUSICAL INSTRUMENT AND THESE GREEK AND LATIN BOOKS.

YOU TAKE THE LUTE,* AND YOU, CAMBIO, THE BOOKS. MY SERVANT WILL LEAD YOU TO MY DAUGHTERS.

* a stringed instrument like a small guitar

A SERVANT LED THE "TEACHERS" AWAY. BAPTISTA TURNED TO HIS GUESTS.

LET US WALK IN THE GARDEN, AND THEN GO TO DINNER! YOU ARE ALL MOST WELCOME!

SIGNIOR BAPTISTA, I CANNOT COME COURTING EVERY DAY. YOU KNEW MY FATHER WELL. AND I AM HEIR* TO ALL HIS LANDS AND GOODS.

IF I WIN YOUR DAUGHTER'S LOVE, WHAT DOWRY WILL COME WITH HER AS MY WIFE?

TWENTY THOUSAND CROWNS,** AND AFTER MY DEATH, ONE-HALF OF MY LANDS. BUT FIRST SHE MUST AGREE TO MARRY YOU!

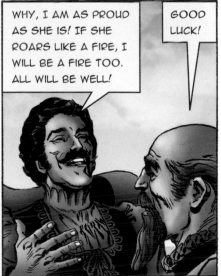

WHY, I AM AS PROUD AS SHE IS! IF SHE ROARS LIKE A FIRE, I WILL BE A FIRE TOO. ALL WILL BE WELL!

GOOD LUCK!

* one who receives money or property after someone's death

** gold coins

JUST THEN HORTENSIO RUSHED INTO THE ROOM.

WELL, WILL MY DAUGHTER BE A MUSICIAN?

I THINK SHE'D MAKE A BETTER SOLDIER!

WHEN I CORRECTED MISS KATHERINA'S PLAYING, SHE BROKE THE LUTE OVER MY HEAD. THEN SHE DROVE ME AWAY WITH BAD NAMES!

WHAT A WOMAN! I CAN'T WAIT TO MEET HER!

COME WITH ME TO MY YOUNGER DAUGHTER. SHE WILL BE THANKFUL FOR YOUR TEACHING!

PETRUCHIO, WILL YOU GO WITH US, OR SHALL I SEND KATHERINA HERE?

I WILL WAIT HERE FOR HER. . . AND COURT HER WITH SPIRIT WHEN SHE ARRIVES.

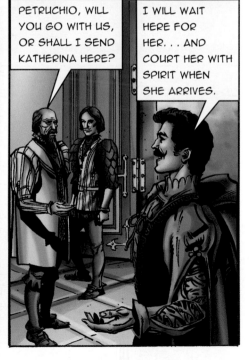

LEFT ALONE, PETRUCHIO PLANNED WHAT HE WOULD SAY TO KATHERINA.

IF SHE SCOLDS, I'LL TELL HER SHE SINGS AS SWEETLY AS A SONGBIRD.

WHEN SHE FROWNS, I'LL SAY HER FACE IS SWEET AS ROSES WASHED WITH DEW!

IF SHE REFUSES TO MARRY ME, I'LL SET A WEDDING DATE AS IF SHE HAD AGREED!

THEN KATHERINA CAME IN.

GOOD DAY, KATE, FOR THAT'S YOUR NAME, I HEAR.

THOSE THAT TALK OF ME CALL ME KATHERINA!

OH, NO! THEY CALL YOU PLAIN KATE— AND PRETTY KATE—AND SOMETIMES KATE THE SHREW!

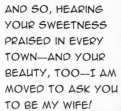

AND SO, HEARING YOUR SWEETNESS PRAISED IN EVERY TOWN—AND YOUR BEAUTY, TOO—I AM MOVED TO ASK YOU TO BE MY WIFE!

THEN LET WHOEVER MOVED YOU HERE MOVE YOU AWAY AGAIN!

COME, SWEET KATE! I WILL MARRY YOU, FOR I AM A GENTLEMAN!

YOU THINK SO?

I SWEAR I'LL HIT YOU BACK IF YOU STRIKE ME AGAIN!

IF YOU STRIKE ME, YOU ARE NO GENTLEMAN!

TAKE THAT!

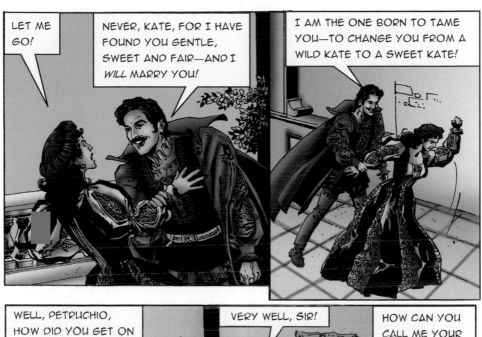

LET ME GO!

NEVER, KATE, FOR I HAVE FOUND YOU GENTLE, SWEET AND FAIR—AND I *WILL* MARRY YOU!

I AM THE ONE BORN TO TAME YOU—TO CHANGE YOU FROM A WILD KATE TO A SWEET KATE!

WELL, PETRUCHIO, HOW DID YOU GET ON WITH MY DAUGHTER?

VERY WELL, SIR!

HOW CAN YOU CALL ME YOUR DAUGHTER?

HAVE YOU SHOWN A FATHER'S LOVE, WISHING ME WED TO THIS CRAZY MAN?

DON'T LISTEN TO HER, SIR! KATHERINA IS JUST PUTTING ON AN ACT. THOSE WHO CALL HER A SHREW ARE SADLY MISTAKEN!

IN FACT, WE SO WELL AGREE THAT WE WILL BE MARRIED NEXT SUNDAY!

YOU *WILL?*

I'LL SEE YOU *HANGED* ON SUNDAY FIRST!

DON'T WORRY. WE'VE AGREED THAT SHE WILL CONTINUE TO ACT LIKE THAT IN PUBLIC. BUT SHE LOVES ME!

SHE *DOES?*

WHEN WE ARE ALONE, YOU WOULD NOT BELIEVE HOW SWEET SHE IS, HANGING ABOUT MY NECK AND KISSING ME!

ORDER A FEAST AND INVITE THE GUESTS. WE WILL BE MARRIED ON SUNDAY!

I DON'T KNOW WHAT TO SAY. . . BUT I WISH YOU JOY!

AT THIS, KATHERINA STORMED OUT OF THE ROOM. PETRUCHIO ALSO LEFT, SAYING THAT HE HAD WEDDING CLOTHES TO BUY.

GOOD LUCK TO YOU BOTH!

WE WILL BE WITNESSES* AT YOUR WEDDING.

ONCE PETRUCHIO HAD GONE, GREMIO TURNED TO BAPTISTA.

THIS IS THE DAY WE HAVE WAITED FOR. YOUR KATHERINA WILL BE MARRIED. WHAT OF YOUR YOUNGER DAUGHTER?

I AM YOUR NEIGHBOR, AND WAS THE FIRST TO COURT BIANCA!

BUT I AM THE ONE WHO LOVES HER MOST!

YOUNGSTER, YOU CAN NEVER LOVE HER AS WELL AS I!

WAIT, GENTLEMEN! I WILL SETTLE THIS!

* observers, people who will swear that an event took place

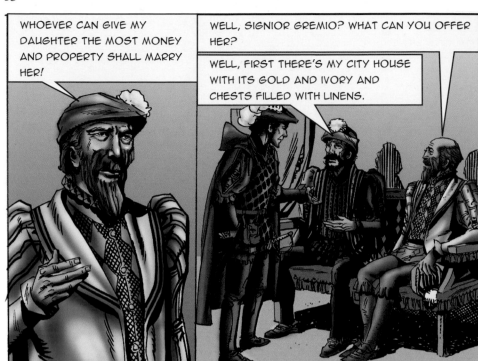

WHOEVER CAN GIVE MY DAUGHTER THE MOST MONEY AND PROPERTY SHALL MARRY HER!

WELL, SIGNIOR GREMIO? WHAT CAN YOU OFFER HER?

WELL, FIRST THERE'S MY CITY HOUSE WITH ITS GOLD AND IVORY AND CHESTS FILLED WITH LINENS.

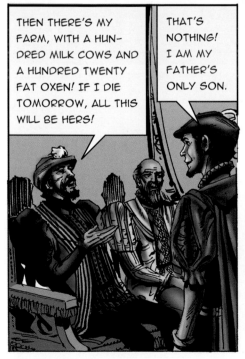

THEN THERE'S MY FARM, WITH A HUNDRED MILK COWS AND A HUNDRED TWENTY FAT OXEN! IF I DIE TOMORROW, ALL THIS WILL BE HERS!

THAT'S NOTHING! I AM MY FATHER'S ONLY SON.

I'LL LEAVE BIANCA THREE OF FOUR HOUSES AS GOOD AS OLD GREMIO'S—PLUS 2,000 DUCATS* YEARLY INCOME** FROM FRUITFUL LAND.

TWO THOUSAND DUCATS! ALL MY LAND DOES NOT BRING IN SO MUCH!

* gold coins

** money received from a job or investment

BUT I WILL GIVE HER MY BIG MERCHANT SHIP* NOW IN THE HARBOR!

MY FATHER HAS THREE GREAT MERCHANT SHIPS, AND SEVERAL SMALLER ONES. BIANCA SHALL HAVE THEM. . . AND TWICE AS MUCH WHATEVER YOU OFFER!

I'VE OFFERED ALL I HAVE! THERE IS NO MORE.

THEN BIANCA IS MINE—BY YOUR PROMISE!

YES, IF YOUR FATHER CONFIRMS YOUR OFFER.

OTHERWISE, IF YOU SHOULD DIE BEFORE HE DOES, WHAT WOULD HAPPEN TO BIANCA'S DOWRY?

BUT HE IS OLD! I AM YOUNG!

MAY NOT YOUNG MEN DIE, AS WELL AS OLD ONES?

NEXT SUNDAY, KATHERINA WILL BE WED. THE SUNDAY FOLLOWING, BIANCA WILL BE MARRIED TO YOU—IF YOUR FATHER BACKS UP YOUR OFFER—TO GREMIO, IF HE DOES NOT!

* trading ship

THANK YOU GENTLEMEN, AND GOODBYE.

WAIT, NEIGHBOR, I WILL GO WITH YOU.

HM. . . IF I WANT TO HELP MY MASTER, I MUST FIND A "SUP-POSED"* FATHER TO BACK UP HIS "SUPPOSED" SON.

DURING THE WEEK THAT FOLLOWED, THE SUPPOSED CAMBIO AND LICIO GAVE LESSONS TO BIANCA.

HIC IBAT SIMOIS; HIC EST SIGEIA TELLUS.**

THE GIRL HAS STUDIED ENOUGH LATIN. IT'S TIME FOR A MUSIC LESSON!

WE'LL FINISH HERE WHILE YOU TUNE YOUR LUTE.

HIC IBAT SIMOIS; I AM LUCENTIO, SON OF VINCENTIO OF PISA, SIGEIA TELLUS, I AM HERE HOP-ING TO WIN YOUR LOVE!

I'LL TRY IT. HIC IBAT SIMOIS, I DON'T KNOW IF I TRUST YOU; SIGEIA TELLUS; DON'T LET LICIO HEAR US!

* make-believe

** a line from the Roman poet Ovid; it means, "Here flowed the Simois (River); here is the Sigeian land."

LICIO (HORTENSIO) USED MUSIC IN THE SAME WAY TO TELL BIANCA HIS TRUE NAME AND HIS PURPOSE. THEN ON SATURDAY. . .

MISS, YOUR FATHER ASKS THAT YOU HELP PREPARE FOR YOUR SISTER'S WEDDING TOMORROW.

OH, YES! I MUST LEAVE.

AND THE WEDDING DAY ARRIVED!

I TOLD YOU HE WAS A FOOL!

THIS IS THE TIME, BUT WHERE IS MY SON-IN-LAW? WILL WE STAND BEFORE THE PRIEST WITH NO BRIDEGROOM?

HE SETS THE DAY, INVITES FRIENDS, YET NEVER MEANS TO MARRY!

THEY'LL POINT AT ME AND SAY, "THERE'S MAD PETRUCHIO'S WIFE. . . IF HE WOULD PLEASE TO COME AND MARRY HER!"

NO, NO SOMETHING HAS KEPT HIM AWAY! PETRUCHIO MEANS WELL! HE MAKES JOKES, BUT HE IS HONEST!

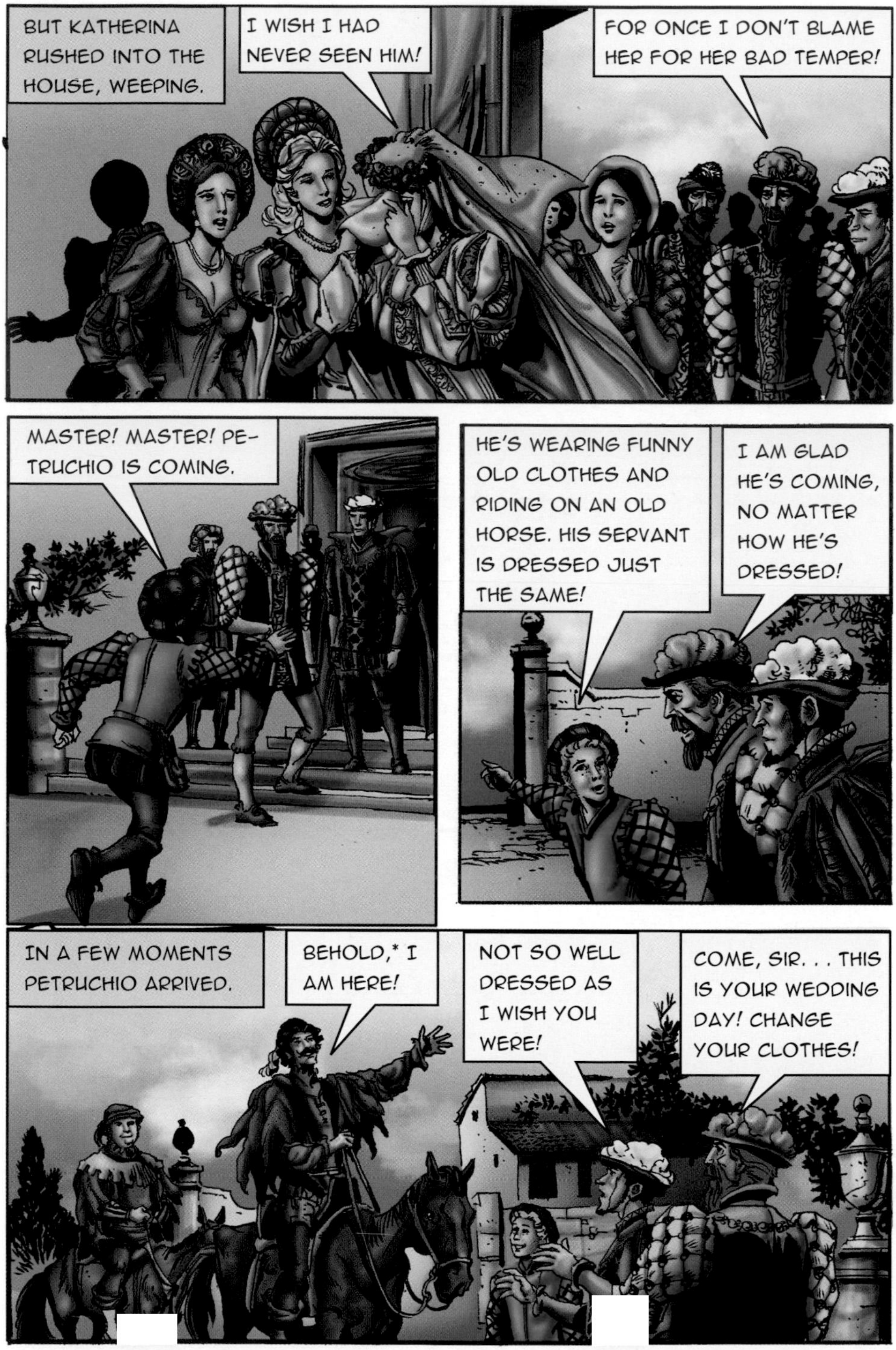
BUT KATHERINA RUSHED INTO THE HOUSE, WEEPING.
I WISH I HAD NEVER SEEN HIM!
FOR ONCE I DON'T BLAME HER FOR HER BAD TEMPER!
MASTER! MASTER! PETRUCHIO IS COMING.
HE'S WEARING FUNNY OLD CLOTHES AND RIDING ON AN OLD HORSE. HIS SERVANT IS DRESSED JUST THE SAME!
I AM GLAD HE'S COMING, NO MATTER HOW HE'S DRESSED!
IN A FEW MOMENTS PETRUCHIO ARRIVED.
BEHOLD,* I AM HERE!
NOT SO WELL DRESSED AS I WISH YOU WERE!
COME, SIR. . . THIS IS YOUR WEDDING DAY! CHANGE YOUR CLOTHES!

* Look!

GO TO MY ROOM. PUT ON SOME OF MY CLOTHES.

NOT I! KATE WILL BE MARRIED TO ME, NOT TO MY CLOTHES.

I MUST FIND MY LOVELY BRIDE. . . THEN IT'S ON TO THE WEDDING!

AT THE CHURCH, PETRUCHIO CONTINUED HIS STRANGE BEHAVIOR.*

HE SHOUTED OUT HIS WEDDING VOWS. . .

HE KNOCKED THE PRIEST TO THE FLOOR. . .

HE EVEN FRIGHTENED HIS BRIDE!

ALL AGREED THAT SUCH A MAD WEDDING WAS NEVER SEEN BEFORE!

* actions

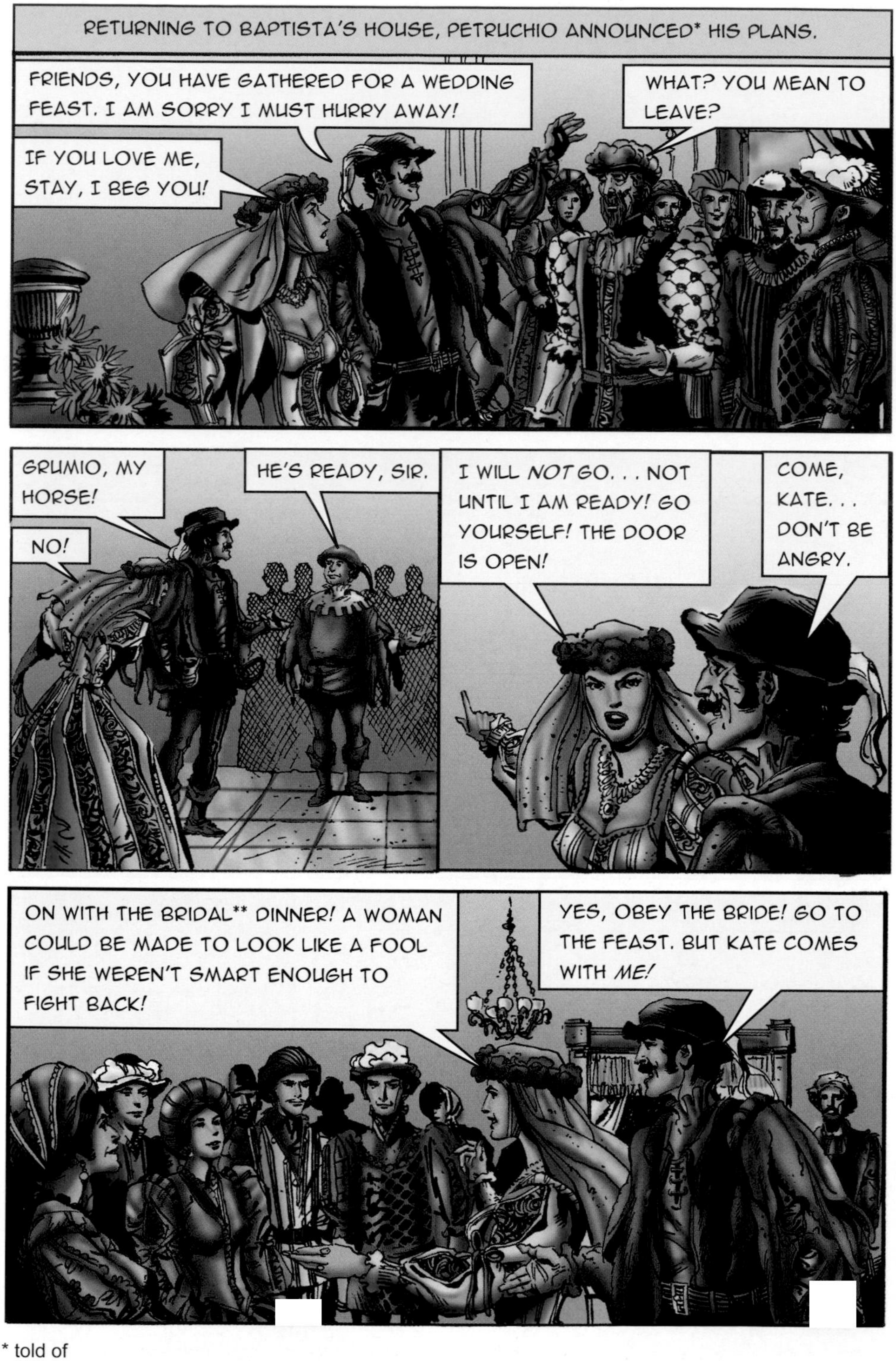
RETURNING TO BAPTISTA'S HOUSE, PETRUCHIO ANNOUNCED* HIS PLANS.
FRIENDS, YOU HAVE GATHERED FOR A WEDDING FEAST. I AM SORRY I MUST HURRY AWAY!
WHAT? YOU MEAN TO LEAVE?
IF YOU LOVE ME, STAY, I BEG YOU!
GRUMIO, MY HORSE!
HE'S READY, SIR.
NO!
I WILL *NOT* GO. . . NOT UNTIL I AM READY! GO YOURSELF! THE DOOR IS OPEN!
COME, KATE. . . DON'T BE ANGRY.
ON WITH THE BRIDAL** DINNER! A WOMAN COULD BE MADE TO LOOK LIKE A FOOL IF SHE WEREN'T SMART ENOUGH TO FIGHT BACK!
YES, OBEY THE BRIDE! GO TO THE FEAST. BUT KATE COMES WITH *ME!*

* told of

** wedding

I WILL BE MASTER OF WHAT BELONGS TO ME! WHO DARES TO STOP ME? GRUMIO, DRAW YOUR SWORD!

FEAR NOT, DEAR KATE! NO ONE SHALL TOUCH YOU! COME ALONG!

HELP!

HAD THEY NOT GONE, I WOULD HAVE DIED LAUGHING!

OF ALL MAD MATCHES, NEVER WAS ONE LIKE THIS!

MY SISTER, BEING MAD HERSELF, IS MADLY MATED!*

AND SO PETRUCHIO AND KATE TRAVELED TO HIS COUNTRY HOME.

OH! OH!

GRUMIO, YOU FOOL! WHY HAVE YOU PICKED SUCH A POOR HORSE FOR MY WIFE?

* wed, married

* leather straps used for guiding a horse

** rascals

FOOD! FOOD! SIT DOWN KATE, AND WELCOME!

WHAT'S THIS? MUTTON?* IT'S BURNED! HOW DARE YOU SERVE IT TO ME?

PLEASE, HUSBAND, IT'S NOT THAT BAD!

IT WAS BURNED—AND HOT – TEMPERED PEOPLE LIKE US SHOULD NEVER EAT OVERCOOKED MEAT!

WELL, NEVER-MIND. WE'LL EAT TOMORROW. YOUR ROOM IS THIS WAY.

BUT, BUT, HUSBAND. . .

I WILL NOT LET HER EAT OR SLEEP. AND EVERYTHING I DO, I'LL TELL HER I DO IT OUT OF KINDNESS!**

* a roast similar to a leg of lamb

** being sweet and gentle

THIS IS HOW I'LL TEACH HER TO CONTROL HER TEMPER!

HE DIDN'T STOP FOR A MOMENT.

THIS BLANKET IS TOO ROUGH. . . THE PILLOW IS TOO HARD. . . THE BED IS NOT MADE PROPERLY!

PETRUCHIO PULLED KATE'S BED TO PIECES. HE SCOLDED THE SERVANTS ALL NIGHT.

MEANWHILE, IN PADUA, TRANIO AND HORTENSIO TALKED ABOUT BIANCA.

WHAT? YOU THINK BIANCA LOVES SOMEONE ELSE?

YES, I DO. STAY OUT OF SIGHT AND WATCH HER WITH THIS TUTOR* CAMBIO!

AND AS BIANCA AND "CAMBIO" WALKED IN THE GARDEN. . .

WHAT I WANT TO TEACH YOU IS THE ART OF LOVE!

I'M SURE YOU ARE MASTER OF THAT ART!

* teacher

I AM HORTENSIO, A GENTLEMAN, NOT A MUSICIAN! I'LL NO LONGER COURT A MAID WHO FAVORS A LOW-BORN* TUTOR!

YOU ARE RIGHT! LET US SWEAR THAT NEITHER OF US WILL WED BIANCA!

HERE'S MY HAND ON IT! INSTEAD, I'LL MARRY A RICH WIDOW WHO LOVES ME! KINDNESS IS BETTER THAN BEAUTY!

AND I'LL NOT MARRY BIANCA, EVEN IF SHE SHOULD BEG ME!

AT THIS, HORTENSIO LEFT, AND TRANIO JOINED BIANCA AND THE REAL LUCENTIO.

BLESS YOU, MISS BIANCA! HORTENSIO AND I HAVE DECIDED NOT TO MARRY YOU.

THEN I CAN MARRY HER! ALL WE NEED IS A MAKE-BELIEVE FATHER TO TALK TO BAPTISTA!

I'VE FOUND HIM! HE'S AN OLD SCHOOLTEACHER. HE EVEN *LOOKS* LIKE VINCENTIO!

GOOD! I'LL DRESS HIM UP, TELL HIM WHAT TO SAY, AND YOUR MARRIAGE WILL BE GUARANTEED!**

* someone not of the noble class

** certain, sure

MEANWHILE, AT PETRUCHIO'S HOME, THE "TAMING" CONTINUED.

TRANIO TOOK THE OLD MAN HOME AND TAUGHT HIM TO PLAY THE PART OF LUCENTIO'S FATHER.

I AM STARVED FOR FOOD, DIZZY FOR LACK OF SLEEP. . . AND ALL IN THE NAME OF LOVE! PLEASE, GRUMIO, BRING ME SOME FOOD!

I DARE NOT, FOR MY LIFE!

MY LOVE, I HAVE PREPARED SOME FOOD FOR YOU MYSELF AND BROUGHT IT HERE.

THEN, GIVE IT TO ME!

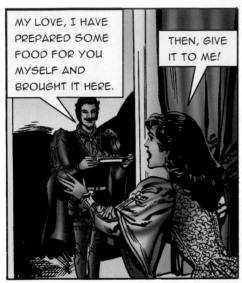

EVEN THE POOREST SERVICE IS REPAID WITH THANKS! SO SHALL MINE BE.

I THANK YOU, SIR.

AND NOW, MY LOVE. . . I HAVE ORDERED YOU SOME CLOTHES FOR YOUR SISTER'S WEDDING.

HERE IS THE CAP YOU WANTED, SIR.

WHY, IT'S MADE LIKE A CEREAL BOWL! IT'S FOOLISH. . . A BABY'S CAP! AWAY WITH IT!

IT LIKE IT!

IT'S THE STYLE! GENTLEWOMEN* WEAR SUCH CAPS.

WHEN *YOU* ARE GENTLE YOU SHALL HAVE ONE TOO—AND NOT TILL THEN!

THIS IS THE DRESS? IT'S TERRIBLE! SLEEVES LIKE CANNONS. . . CUT UP LIKE AN APPLE TART! TAKE IT AWAY!

BUT THIS IS WHAT THEY'RE WEARING NOW!

BUT COME, MY KATE! WE WILL GO TO YOUR FATHER'S IN OUR OLD CLOTHES! OUR PURSES WILL BE PROUD AND OUR CLOTHES POOR!

* women of the noble class

LET'S SEE. . . IT'S EARLY MORNING NOW. WE SHALL EASILY REACH PADUA BY DINNERTIME.

BUT, SIR. . . IT IS ALMOST TWO O'CLOCK! IT WILL BE SUPPERTIME BEFORE WE GET THERE!

WHATEVER I SAY, OR DO, OR THINK, YOU CONTRADICT* ME! THEN I WON'T GO TODAY! AND WHEN I *DO* GO, IT WILL BE WHAT TIME I SAY IT IS!

MEANWHILE, IN PADUA, TRANIO TOOK HIS MAKE-BELIEVE FATHER TO MEET BAPTISTA, WHO STILL BELIEVED TRANIO TO BE THE REAL LUCENTIO.

SIGNIOR BAPTISTA, HERE IS MY FATHER, VINCENTIO.

SINCE MY SON AND YOUR DAUGHTER LOVE EACH OTHER, I AM WILLING TO LET THEM MARRY.

SIR, I AM WELL PLEASED!

LET US GO TO MY HOUSE TO SIGN THE PAPERS. I'LL SEND FOR A CLERK. SEND YOUR SERVANT TO BRING YOUR DAUGHTER THERE.

GO, CAMBIO!

MOST GLADLY SIR!

SO TRANIO AND BAPTISTA LEFT FOR TRANIO'S LODGINGS.** THE REAL LUCENTIO HURRIED TO BIANCA WITH BIONDELLO FOLLOWING ALONG.

* argue with; say the opposite of what another is saying

** a rented room or house

CAMBIO! WAIT! MY MASTER SENDS ME WITH ORDERS FOR YOU.

WHAT ARE THEY?

WHILE BAPTISTA IS SAFE WITH TRANIO, YOU MUST TAKE BIANCA TO THE OLD PRIEST WHO WAITS FOR YOU AT ST. LUKE'S CHURCH!

TO MARRY HER? WILL SHE BE WILLING? WHY NOW?

BECAUSE AT ANY TIME OUR PLANS MAY BE FOUND OUT AND YOU MAY LOSE HER!

THEN I'LL DO IT! AND I KNOW MY BIANCA WILL AGREE!

THAT SAME DAY, PETRUCHIO AND KATHERINA HAD BEGUN THE TRIP TO BAPTISTA'S HOUSE.

SEE HOW BRIGHT THE MOON SHINES!

THE MOON? IT IS THE SUN! IT IS NOT MOONLIGHT NOW!

I SAY IT IS THE *MOON!* IT SHALL BE THE MOON, OR STARS, OR WHATEVER I CHOOSE, OR WE WON'T GO TO YOUR FATHER'S HOUSE!

THEN LET US GO. IT SHALL BE SUN, OR MOON, OR WHATEVER YOU PLEASE!

CALL IT A CANDLE IF YOU WISH! AND WHATEVER YOU CALL IT, I WILL CALL IT TOO.

THEN LET US GO FORWARD!

ON THE WAY, KATHERINA AND PETRUCHIO MET AN OLD GENTLEMAN.

GOOD DAY, MISS. TELL ME, KATE, HAVE YOU EVER SEEN SUCH A BEAUTIFUL FACE AS THIS YOUNG GIRL'S?

INDEED, SHE IS LOVELY. HAPPY THE PARENTS OF SUCH A BEAUTIFUL CHILD!

COME KATE, I HOPE YOU ARE NOT MAD! THIS IS A MAN, OLD AND WRINKLED!

WHY, I BEG YOUR PARDON. THE SUN MUST HAVE BLINDED ME! NOW I SEE. INDEED HE IS AN OLD GENTLEMAN!

IF YOU ARE GOING OUR WAY, WE'LL BE GLAD OF YOUR COMPANY.

I AM VICENTIO OF PISA, I AM BOUND FOR PADUA TO VISIT MY SON, LUCENTIO.

THEN WE ARE TRULY RELATED. YOUR SON, LUCENTIO, IS MARRYING MY WIFE'S SISTER!

IS THIS SO?

SHE IS A WORTHY WIFE FOR YOUR SON, WELL BROUGHT-UP, WITH A GOOD DOWRY.

AND THEY WILL BE HAPPY TO SEE YOU!

THEN THIS IS INDEED A HAPPY MEETING!

WHEN THEY REACHED PADUA. . .

WE WILL LEAVE YOU HERE. THIS IS LUCENTIO'S HOUSE.

NO, NO! YOU MUST COME IN AND HAVE A DRINK BEFORE YOU GO!

WHO'S BREAKING DOWN THE GATE?

PLEASE TELL LUCENTIO THAT HIS FATHER IS HERE AT THE DOOR!

YOU LIE! I AM HIS FATHER LOOKING OUT THE WINDOW!

YOU ARE HIS FATHER?

SO HIS MOTHER SAYS, IF I MAY BELIEVE HER!

COME, NOW! IT IS WRONG TO TAKE ANOTHER MAN'S NAME!

OH-OH! IT'S MY OLD MASTER, VINCENTIO! NOW WE ARE IN TROUBLE!

BIONDELLO, COME HERE! HAVE YOU FORGOTTEN ME?

HELP! HERE'S A MADMAN WHO'LL MURDER ME!

HELP, SON! HELP, SIGNIOR BAPTISTA!

LET'S STAND ASIDE, KATE, AND SEE HOW THIS ENDS.

WHO ARE YOU, SIR, WHO TRIES TO BEAT MY SERVANT?

NO, WHO ARE *YOU*—DRESSED IN MY SON'S CLOTHES? YOU HAVE MURDERED HIM!

YOU ARE WRONG, SIR! WHAT DO YOU THINK IS HIS NAME?

HE IS TRANIO, MY SON'S SERVANT, RAISED BY ME SINCE HE WAS THREE YEARS OLD!

YOU ARE MAD! HIS NAME IS LUCENTIO AND HE IS MY SON!

CALL A POLICE-MAN! TAKE THIS MADMAN TO JAIL!

JUST THEN BIONDELLO RETURNED WITH BIANCA AND THE REAL LUCENTIO.

NOW WE ARE RUINED!

MY SON—YOU ARE ALIVE!

PARDON ME, DEAR FATHER.

BUT... WHERE IS LUCENTIO?

HERE I AM. THE RIGHT LUCENTIO, SON OF THE RIGHT VINCENTIO, AND WHO HAS JUST MARRIED YOUR DAUGHTER!

BUT... IS THIS NOT MY CAMBIO?

CAMBIO IS CHANGED INTO LUCENTIO.

I MADE TRANIO CHANGE PLACES WITH ME! PARDON HIM, DEAR FATHER, FOR MY SAKE!

LET US GO INSIDE, BAPTISTA. TOGETHER WE WILL MAKE A PROPER MARRIAGE AGREEMENT* BETWEEN OUR CHILDREN.

* contract

EVERYONE HURRIED AWAY. ONLY KATE AND PETRUCHIO WERE LEFT ON THE STREET.

HUSBAND, LET'S FOLLOW THEM TO SEE THE END OF THIS!

FIRST KISS ME, KATE, AND THEN WE WILL.

WHAT? HERE IN THE STREET?

ARE YOU ASHAMED OF ME?

OH, NO, ONLY ASHAMED TO KISS!

THEN LET US GO HOME AGAIN!

NO, I WILL KISS YOU.

COME, SWEET KATE! LOVE ARRIVES BETTER LATE THAN NEVER!

NOT LONG AFTERWARD, THREE NEWLY-MARRIED COUPLES MET FOR A BANQUET* AT LUCENTIO'S HOUSE.

BROTHER PETRUCHIO, SISTER KATHERINA. . . YOU, HORTENSIO, WITH YOUR LOVING WIDOW. . . WELCOME TO OUR HOUSE!

WHEN THE MEAL WAS OVER, THE LADIES LEFT, AND THE MEN TALKED AMONG THEMSELVES.

LET'S HAVE A TOAST!**

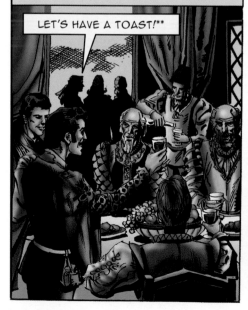

SOON THE TALK TURNED TO THE NEW BRIDES.

TRUTH TO TELL, SON PE-TRUCHIO, I FEAR YOU'VE MARRIED A SHREW!

I SAY NO! I'LL PROVE IT WITH A BET!

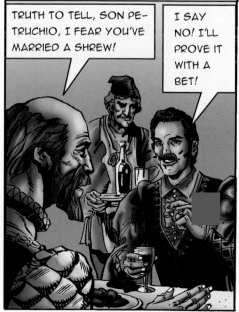

* a large party

** a drink taken in honor of someone

LET EACH ONE OF US SEND FOR HIS WIFE. WHO-EVER ARRIVES FIRST SHALL WIN THE BET FOR HER HUSBAND!

GOOD! WHAT'S THE BET?

TWENTY CROWNS!

I'D BET THAT MUCH ON MY HAWK OR MY HOUND! ON MY WIFE, TWENTY TIMES AS MUCH!

GOOD!

A HUNDRED THEN!

I'LL BEGIN. BIONDELLO, GO ASK YOUR MISTRESS TO COME TO ME.

YES, SIR.

BIONDELLO LEFT, BUT SOON HE RETURNED ALONE.

SIR, SHE SENDS WORD THAT SHE IS TOO BUSY TO COME.

WHAT KIND OF ANSWER IS THAT?

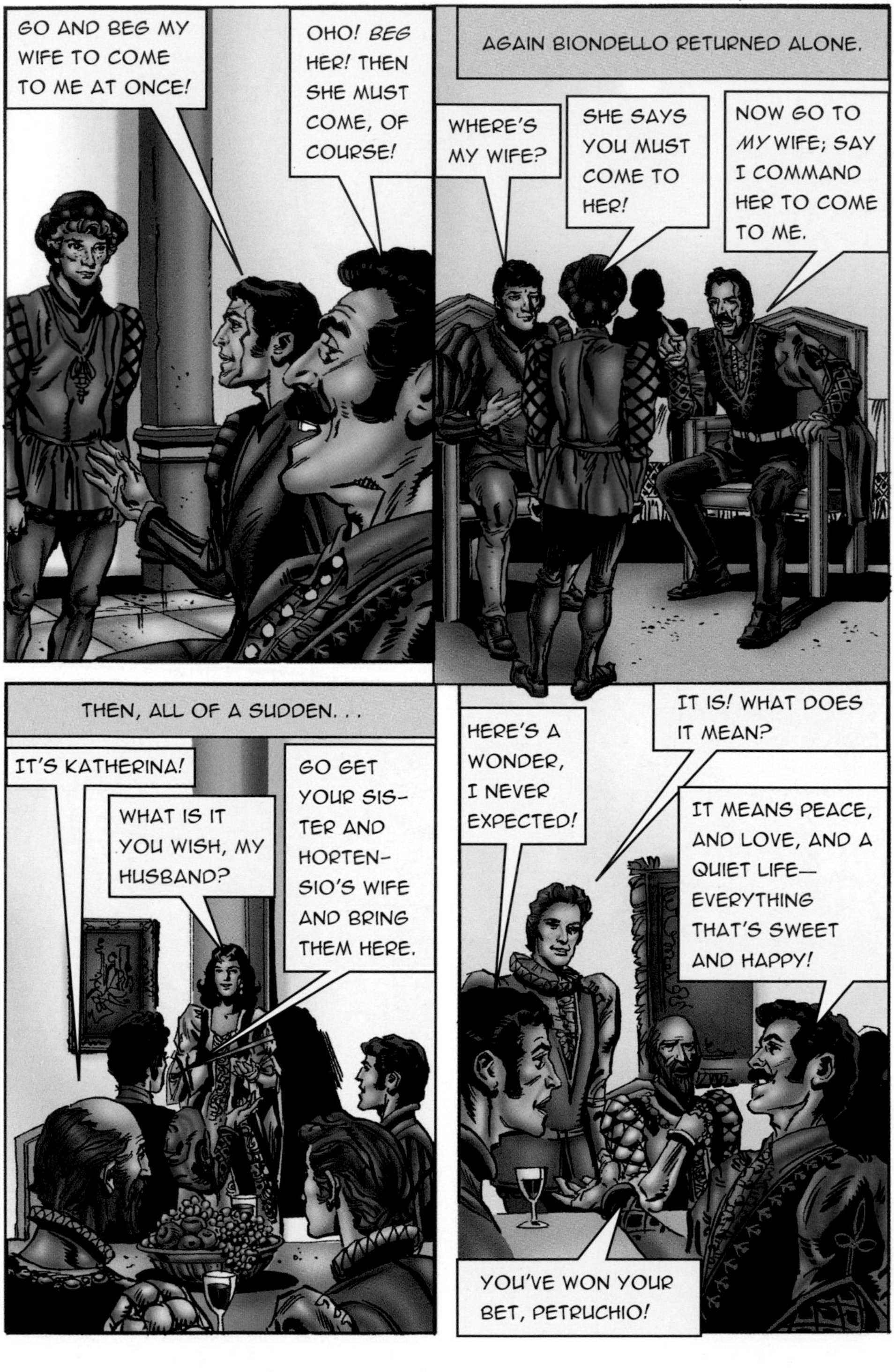
GO AND BEG MY WIFE TO COME TO ME AT ONCE!
OHO! *BEG* HER! THEN SHE MUST COME, OF COURSE!
AGAIN BIONDELLO RETURNED ALONE.
WHERE'S MY WIFE?
SHE SAYS YOU MUST COME TO HER!
NOW GO TO *MY* WIFE; SAY I COMMAND HER TO COME TO ME.
THEN, ALL OF A SUDDEN. . .
IT'S KATHERINA!
WHAT IS IT YOU WISH, MY HUSBAND?
GO GET YOUR SISTER AND HORTENSIO'S WIFE AND BRING THEM HERE.
HERE'S A WONDER, I NEVER EXPECTED!
IT IS! WHAT DOES IT MEAN?
IT MEANS PEACE, AND LOVE, AND A QUIET LIFE— EVERYTHING THAT'S SWEET AND HAPPY!
YOU'VE WON YOUR BET, PETRUCHIO!

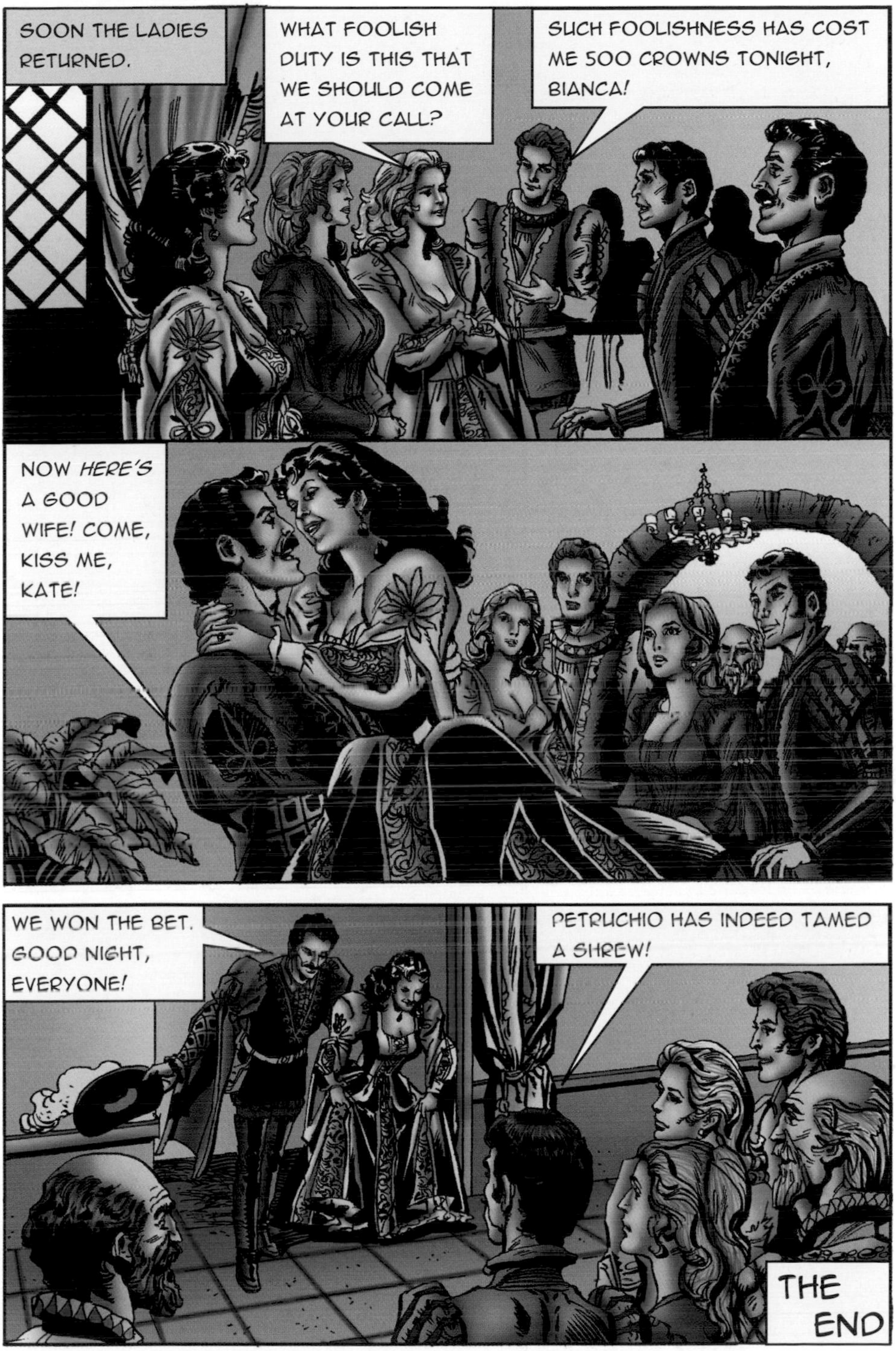
SOON THE LADIES RETURNED.
WHAT FOOLISH DUTY IS THIS THAT WE SHOULD COME AT YOUR CALL?
SUCH FOOLISHNESS HAS COST ME 500 CROWNS TONIGHT, BIANCA!
NOW *HERE'S* A GOOD WIFE! COME, KISS ME, KATE!
WE WON THE BET. GOOD NIGHT, EVERYONE!
PETRUCHIO HAS INDEED TAMED A SHREW!
THE END